Groundwood Books / House of Anansi Press
groundwoodbooks.com

We gratefully acknowledge for their financial support of our publishing
program the Canada Council for the Arts, the Ontario Arts Council and
the Government of Canada.

Canada Council   Conseil des Arts
for the Arts   du Canada

ONTARIO ARTS COUNCIL
CONSEIL DES ARTS DE L'ONTARIO
an Ontario government agency
un organisme du gouvernement de l'Ontario

With the participation of the Government of Canada | Canadä
Avec la participation du gouvernement du Canada

Library and Archives Canada Cataloguing in Publication
Title: Aunt Pearl / Monica Kulling ; [illustrated by] Irene Luxbacher.
Names: Kulling, Monica, author. | Luxbacher, Irene, illustrator.
Identifiers: Canadiana (print) 20189065524 | Canadiana (ebook)
20189065532 | ISBN 9781773061535 (hardcover) |
ISBN 9781773061542 (EPUB) | ISBN 9781773062747 (Kindle)
Classification: LCC PS8571.U54 A96 2019 | DDC jC813/.54—dc23

The art in this book was made with pencil, watercolor and acrylic paint. All
the hand-made drawings and paintings were then scanned and digitally placed.
A print was created for each page, and more drawings and final touches were
added by hand in graphite, colored pencil, found papers and gouache paints.
Design by Sara Loos and Michael Solomon
Printed and bound in Malaysia

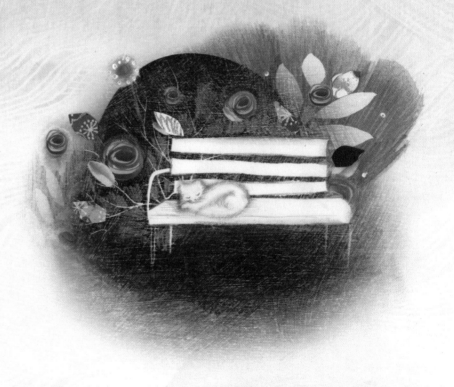

In loving memory of Sheila Barry —
publisher, editor, friend —
forever missed. M.K. + I.L.

Aunt Pearl

WRITTEN BY

Monica Kulling

ILLUSTRATED BY

Irene Luxbacher

Groundwood Books
House of Anansi Press
Toronto Berkeley

Aunt Pearl had no home of her own. She slept wherever she could.

Sometimes she crashed on a friend's couch. Sometimes she holed up in a hostel. In summer, she slept on city benches.

"That's not how it should be," said Mom. "Pearl will live with us."

Dan and Marta had never met their aunt Pearl.
She arrived pushing a loaded shopping cart.
"I'm here!" she shouted. "And I've brought along my
worldly goods. Now, which of you is Dan and which is Marta?"
Aunt Pearl was strange. There was no doubt about it.

A man in a beat-up van arrived with
boxes and bags of more worldly goods.

"Tomorrow's garbage day," hinted Mom.
"I can help you sort things."

"This isn't trash, Rose," Aunt Pearl
replied sharply. "It's my life."

Marta was only six, but she knew a
problem when she saw one.

Aunt Pearl crammed all her stuff into
the garage, the basement and her bedroom.
  "Your bedroom's a mess!" exclaimed Marta.
  "It's packed to the rafters," added Dan.
  "It's organized!" replied Aunt Pearl.

Dan and Marta were used
to fewer things. Mom liked the
house to be neat as a pin, with
nothing out of place.

At dinner Aunt Pearl wore her hat covered with buttons.
"Make yourself at home," said Mom.
Dan and Marta knew that meant, "Please, take off your hat."
Dan read one of the buttons out loud: "Normal people scare me."
"I live by those words," said Aunt Pearl, chewing chicken.

Dan read another: "Keep calm and hop along."
Marta sprang up from her chair and hopped all over the room like a bunny.

Mom said she had a headache and went to get an aspirin.

During the day, Dan and Marta went to summer camp. Dan liked it. He was learning how to use a camera. Marta didn't like it. She wasn't learning anything.

"I'm off to see what passes for trash around here," said Aunt Pearl one morning.

"I'm coming!" yelled Marta, and lickety-split she was out the door.

"She really doesn't like camp," said Dan.

The houses on the street stood side by side, with garbage bins out front.

"Are you homeless?" asked Marta.

Aunt Pearl gave her a look. "I live with you, don't I?"

"I mean before."

Aunt Pearl didn't reply. She was rummaging through a bin. "Well, lookee here!"

Aunt Pearl shoved a doll with scrappy hair and one eye into Marta's face.

"For you," she said.

Marta shrieked. "That doll's creepy."

Aunt Pearl tossed it into her shopping cart.

"Why do you go through garbage?" asked Marta.

"People are forever throwing away perfectly good things," replied Aunt Pearl. "I give stuff a second chance. Like that chair over there."

Marta raced over and plopped into the
kiddie armchair.
"I'm giving this chair a second chance!"
she shouted gleefully.

The two scavengers trekked home with their treasures.

Mom didn't want to give the chair a second chance.

"Mom, pleeeease," whined Marta.

"That filthy chair is not coming into my clean house."

And that was that.

Marta asked Aunt Pearl to come to camp, but she was busy in the garage.

"Maybe tomorrow," she said. "I'm making a present for your mom. If you haven't noticed, we're in the doghouse."

Marta didn't know what that meant.

"It means that if there were a doghouse in your backyard, you and I would be living in it."

Marta thought this was hilarious. She got down on all fours and barked. "Arf! Arf! Arf!"

"You are one strange girl," muttered Aunt Pearl.

The next day at camp, some of the kids laughed at Aunt Pearl, but she didn't notice.

She dumped out a sack of bottle caps.

"You guys are going to help me make a new top for this table."

When Mom saw the wacky table in front of her white couch, she didn't look happy. Then, slowly, she smiled.

"Yay! We don't have to live in the doghouse!" yelled Marta.

When Aunt Pearl wasn't looking for things that needed second chances, she tried to help around the house. Most of the time, that didn't work out. She was hopeless at keeping her room tidy.

Once she tried to cook dinner, but hot dogs and
baked beans weren't Mom's idea of a healthy meal.

As summer began to think about turning into fall,
Aunt Pearl grew more and more quiet. She didn't bother much
with garbage days anymore.

Every week Marta brought out her wagon. "I'm ready
to give things a second chance."

But Aunt Pearl just stared into the ravine at the bottom
of the yard where the trees grew tangled and green.

Marta knew when someone wanted to be alone.

One night Aunt Pearl woke the whole house. She was outside,
pacing and talking to herself.

"What's the matter, Pearl?" asked Mom gently. "It's three
in the morning."

"Did you have a bad dream?" asked Marta, taking her
aunt's hand.

"I've had many of those, sweet girl," said Aunt Pearl, softly
patting Marta's head.

One morning Aunt Pearl didn't come to breakfast.
"Why'd she go?" asked Dan tearfully. "She left her stuff."
Marta was quiet. She knew a mystery when she met one.
She also knew she would miss Aunt Pearl on garbage days,
and every other day, too.